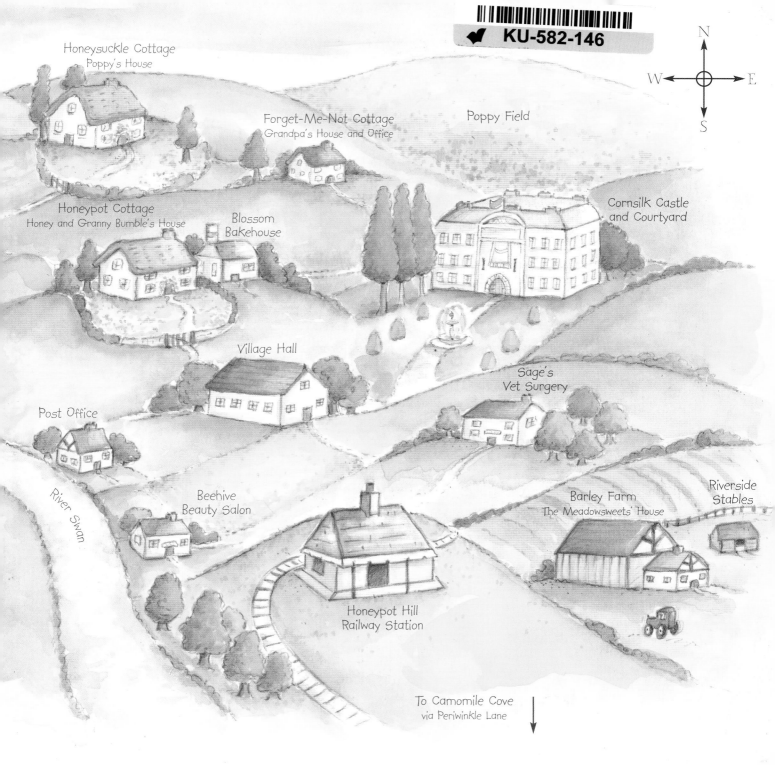

Honeysuckle Cottage
Poppy's House

Forget-Me-Not Cottage
Grandpa's House and Office

Poppy Field

KU-582-146

N
W ✦ E
S

Honeypot Cottage
Honey and Granny Bumble's House

Blossom
Bakehouse

Cornsilk Castle
and Courtyard

Village Hall

Sage's
Vet Surgery

Post Office

Beehive
Beauty Salon

Barley Farm
The Meadowsweets' House

Riverside
Stables

River Swan

Honeypot Hill
Railway Station

To Camomile Cove
via Periwinkle Lane

Join Princess Poppy on more adventures . . .

★ The Birthday ★ Ballet Shoes ★ The Fair Day Ball
★ Twinkletoes ★ The Wedding ★ The Play
★ Poppy's Secret Christmas ★ The Baby Twins
★ Petals and Picnics – A Make-and-Do Book
★ Puzzle and Play – A Sticker Activity Book
★ A True Princess ★ Pocket Money Princess

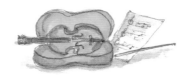

FRIENDS TOGETHER
A PICTURE CORGI BOOK 978 0 552 55984 3

First published in Great Britain by Picture Corgi,
an imprint of Random House Children's Books

This edition published 2007

Text copyright © Janey Louise Jones, 2007
Illustration copyright © Picture Corgi Books, 2007
Illustrations by Veronica Vasylenko
Design by Tracey Cunnell

Picture Corgi Books are published by Random House Children's Books,
61–63 Uxbridge Road, London W5 5SA, a division of The Random House Group Ltd,
in Australia by Random House Australia (Pty) Ltd, 20 Alfred Street, Milsons Point, Sydney, NSW 2061, Australia,
in New Zealand by Random House New Zealand Ltd, 18 Poland Road, Glenfield, Auckland 10, New Zealand,
in South Africa by Random House (Pty) Ltd, Isle of Houghton,
Corner Boundary Road & Carse O'Gowrie, Houghton 2198, South Africa
in India by Random House Publishers India Private Limited 301 World Trade Tower,
Hotel Intercontinental Grand Complex, Barakhamba Lane, New Delhi 110 001, India
THE RANDOM HOUSE GROUP Limited Reg. No. 954009
www.kidsatrandomhouse.co.uk
www.princesspoppy.com

A CIP catalogue record for this book is available from the British Library.

Printed in China

Friends Together

Written by Janey Louise Jones

PICTURE CORGI

For the real Abigail,
with thanks for your support

★

Friends Together

featuring

Mum
★

Hector Melody
★

Princess Poppy

Abigail Melody
★

Natasha Melody
★

Angel
★

Archie
★

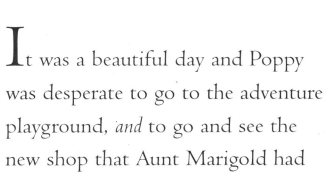

It was a beautiful day and Poppy was desperate to go to the adventure playground, *and* to go and see the new shop that Aunt Marigold had told her about, but Mum was taking ages to get the twins ready.

"Muuuuuum! I'm ready!" called Poppy impatiently from the garden wall.

"All right, Poppy! I'm coming," sighed Mum, as she pushed the pram out of the front door.

When they reached the new shop, Poppy gasped — it was amazing, full of every sort of musical instrument imaginable. They walked in and saw a man and woman behind the counter and a little girl playing a beautiful lullaby on the piano.

"Good morning," said Mum. "I'm Lavender Cotton, and this is Poppy, Angel and Archie."

"Hello!" replied the man.

"We're on our way to the adventure playground at Cornsilk Castle," explained Mum, "but we thought we'd pop in and welcome you to Honeypot Hill first. I'm sure you'll love it here."

"Thank you!" he replied. "And welcome to Melody Makers Music Shop! I'm Hector Melody and this is my wife, Natasha and our daughter, Abigail."

£110

£75

VIOLIN LESSONS

HANDMADE GUITARS

PLAY THE FLUTE

LEARN TO SING
ask for details

SINGER
wanted for
new band

PIANO
FOR SA

Natasha and Abigail smiled warmly at them. Poppy smiled right back. She thought Abigail looked really nice and she wished she could play the piano as well as her. But Poppy had only just started piano lessons.

"We're having an opening party later this afternoon," said Natasha, as she handed Mum a flier. "Please come and do bring along anyone you like – the more the merrier."

"Thank you," said Mum. "We'd love to, wouldn't we Poppy?"

"Yes, please!" smiled Poppy.

"We'd better go to the adventure playground now or we won't have time to get ready for the party!" said Mum. "Maybe Abigail would like to come with us – we'll drop her back on our way home."

Abigail's eyes lit up. "Can I go, Dad? Please?"

Mr Melody looked at the grandfather clock.

"Weeeell," he said. "It is your piano practice time, Abigail. *And* we were going to squeeze in a bit of violin for your exam, weren't we?" Abigail looked disappointed.

"Oh, Hector! Half an hour won't make any difference," said Natasha. "Fresh air will do Abby good."

Mr Melody finally agreed but made Abigail promise that she would do some violin practice before the party.

When they arrived at the adventure playground, Poppy ran towards the swings. By the time Abigail caught up, Poppy was already swinging high in the sky.

"Come on, Abby! See whether you can swing as high as me!" she called.

"I'm not very good at swings!" said Abigail.

"I'm really good at this!" boasted Poppy. "I'll show you how to go high."

"You're brilliant!" agreed Abigail. "I wish I could be as good as you!"

"Let's go on the roundabout now," suggested Poppy. "I can make it go super fast."

"Dad says getting dizzy isn't good for you," said Abigail. "I'm happy just watching you — you're so good at everything."

Poppy liked it when people admired her. It was a nice feeling.

"I can play piano really well too – I'm very musical!" added Poppy, getting a bit carried away. "And I'm good at swinging and horse-riding and ballet *and* other stuff."

"I may not be able to do all those things," said Abigail, who was getting tired of Poppy's bragging now, "but I bet you can't play as many instruments as I can. My dad says I'm as good as a grown-up!"

"Girls, we'd better go in a minute," called Mum, before Poppy had a chance to say anything to Abigail.

"As you're so good on the piano why don't we do a duet together at the party?" suggested Abigail, as Poppy walked her home. Poppy couldn't say no now so she just nodded.

When they got back to Honeysuckle Cottage Poppy was unusually quiet.

Oh no! Why did I lie?

"Mum, I don't want to go to the party any more," Poppy announced.

"Oh, Poppy! Why not?" asked Mum, looking confused. "You and Abigail looked like you were getting on so well. Go and get ready while I change the twins. I'm sure you'll feel more like going when you've put a pretty dress on."

Poppy sat on her bed. She looked at all her lovely clothes. She so wanted to get dressed up, but now she couldn't, all because of her silly lie.

Then Poppy had an idea . . .

If I put a plaster on my finger I can say that it's too sore to play piano but I will still be able to go to the party!

Poppy was feeling much happier now, so she put on her pink party dress, pink shoes and flower hair clips.

Then she got the First Aid kit from the bathroom
and very carefully put two plasters on the
middle finger of her right hand.

"I'm ready to go now," called Poppy.

"Poppy, you look lovely – just like a princess," said Mum as Poppy walked in. "I knew you'd feel better once you had your party clothes on."

But as soon as Mum saw the plasters she wanted to know what had happened to Poppy's finger.

"Um, well, you see. What it is . . ." stammered Poppy.

"Yes?" queried Mum.

"I think I might have a splinter from my dressing-table in it!" lied Poppy for the second time that day.

"Let me have a look," said Mum firmly.

Very slowly, Poppy took off the plaster. Mum looked at Poppy's finger.

"I can't see anything wrong with it, Poppy. *Have* you actually hurt yourself?" demanded Mum.

"Um . . . er . . . no!" she confessed. "It's just that I accidentally told Abigail that I am really good at piano and now she wants me to play a duet with her at the party. I do want to go but I can't play a duet. She's so much better than me and I'll look really silly. I thought if I just . . ."

"Poppy! Do true princesses tell fibs?" asked Mum.

"I'm sorry, Mum. Really I am. I just wanted everyone, especially Abigail, to think I am really good at something, just like she is."

Mum sighed. "You're going to have to tell Abigail the truth, darling. You can only be a true princess again if you can be happy for your friends when they are better at something than you are. Come on, I'll be there if you need me."

The party was in full swing when they arrived at the shop.
"Poppy! Shall we practice our duet now?" asked Abigail
as soon as she saw her new friend.

"Um, Abigail, I am really sorry, but . . . um . . . I'm . . . um . . . not as good at playing the piano as I said I was. I was jealous of how good you are," admitted Poppy. "I just wish I was really great at something."

"But I think you are great!" said Abigail sweetly. "I'm only good at music. You're good at so many fun things. I wish *I* was more like *you* but Dad makes me practise all the time!"

"Maybe you can help me get better at piano and I can teach you some fun games and you can come to my ballet classes and ride Twinkletoes with me — if that's ok with your dad!" suggested Poppy.

"That would be perfect, I'll ask him!" smiled Abigail.

Then Abigail played a lovely piece on the piano and Poppy clapped the loudest of all.

When Abigail finished her piece, she and Poppy held hands and headed off to play with the other children.

As they played, Mum overheard Poppy saying, "You see, I'm not especially good at anything yet, but my mum says I'm a princess . . . when I tell the truth!"

Mum smiled. That wasn't a lie. She was really proud of her little princess.